This Book Belongs To

Aksara P3Y

For my Godchildren – JH
For my family - RC

Published in the UK in 2007 by Starlet Ltd.
Belgrave Business Centre,
Frederick Street, Edinburgh EH2 1EP

Text & Illustrations copyright © Starlet ltd. 2007

Design by Zero Design Ltd.

Printed by Scotprint

ISBN-10   0-9551098-2-5
ISBN-13   978-0-9551098-2-9
EAN   9780955109829

Printed in The United Kingdom of Great Britain and Northern Ireland

Michelle
The Rock Concert

By
Julie Hegarty
Illustrated by Ritchie Collins

To Aksara
with lots of love
xxx

Screech the seagull flew overhead
and noticed Michelle on the ground.
She was hurrying about with Starfish.
Even Hermie was rushing around.
"**Blimey!**" he thought, flapping his wings,
"They look very busy.

But all that to-ing and fro-ing is
making me rather diZzy!"

With both feet tucked up
he went spinning down,
as fast as a jumbo jet.

Then splash!
He crashed right in the pool.
Getting everyone around soaking wet!

"Oh Screech!" gasped Michelle all soggy and dripping, as she tried to regain her composure. "Please look where you're going, you might hurt yourself and try not to tumble me over!"

"Ooops!" Screech replied, "I'll try better next time, but why are you all so excited? I came to see if you needed some help."

"Thank you," said Michelle "I'm delighted."
"A Rock Star is singing in our pool today and
she's coming from across the sand."

"Who is it? Who is it?" he asked Michelle, who replied.

"It's HARMONY and the Slippery Fish Band!"

"I love Harmony!
She's dreamy." Screech said.
"My nest has a full sized poster!

She's the prettiest
creature in the deep
blue sea. I wonder if
I'll get to meet her."

Soon Starfish came over and Hermie too.
The commotion had made them quite curious.
When suddenly
they heard the most
terrible voice and
whoever it was - she
was furious!

"Come on keep up you lazy fish." Harmony shouted as she came into view.

Hermie, being star struck, thrust out his claw blurting, "I can't believe it's you."

"What are you doing?" the Pop Star squealed.
"Don't you know who I am?"
"Oh yes he does," Screech said flying up,
"But **I'm** your number one fan."
The beautiful Anemone stood very tall
with wonderful colours aglow.
She parted her tentacles and
looking around
demanded,

Who's in charge of this show?"

"I am." said Michelle,
"Glad you could come.
We've been working
so hard all day."

"Well? What are you waiting for?"
Harmony replied and pushed her out of the way.
"I need a ledge to sit on," Harmony demanded,
"And fresh seaweed would be good.
And a shade to protect my colourful skin.
And make sure there's plenty of food!"
"You can have my ledge."
said Michelle leading the way,
"It's nice, and really
quite comfy."
"Nice!" Harmony
moaned as she
turned away.
"Huh,
this place is too
small and bumpy."

Screech flew back with some seaweed he'd found, but again got into a flap.

He dived straight in.
And yes, you guessed it,
landed right on Harmony's lap.

"Sorry,"
Screech apologized,
as he brushed her down with his wing.
"Get out of my face." Harmony squealed
"Or I won't be
able to sing!"

Harmony threw herself down and
waving about began to sob and cry.

"All I asked for were simple things,
so why can't I have them?
Oh, why?"

Then Hermie, who'd spent
ages making the food,
rushed to the
scene quite
quickly.

CRABBIT

But Harmony took,
one **long** hard look,
and turned terribly green and sickly.

"Yuck!" she blurted, "Take it away!
Get it out of my sight you fool!"
So Hermie picked up
the tray
and scuttled off to the
other side of the pool.

What Hermie didn't see were
The Slippery Fish Band
who watched him put down the tray.

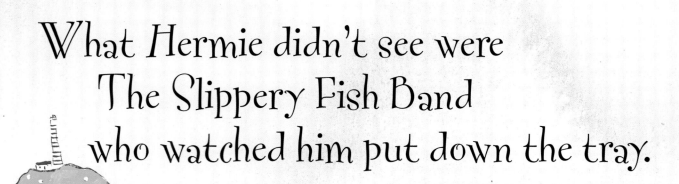

They spied on him and licking their lips,
waited till he walked away.

Then they scoffed all the food.
They ate it all up.
And fell asleep in the
late evening sun.

Meanwhile the fans
gathered to see the show
and Harmony called,
"Places everyone."

But the fish didn't hear.
They couldn't wake up!
Neither drummer, nor bass guitar.

"Where are my guys?" Harmony wailed.
"Is this how they treat me, their star?"

Poor Hermie confessed, "They're fast asleep!
They've eaten up all the food."

"What?"
Exclaimed Harmony,
"You fed the fish?"
Then the crowd
grew impatient
and boOed.

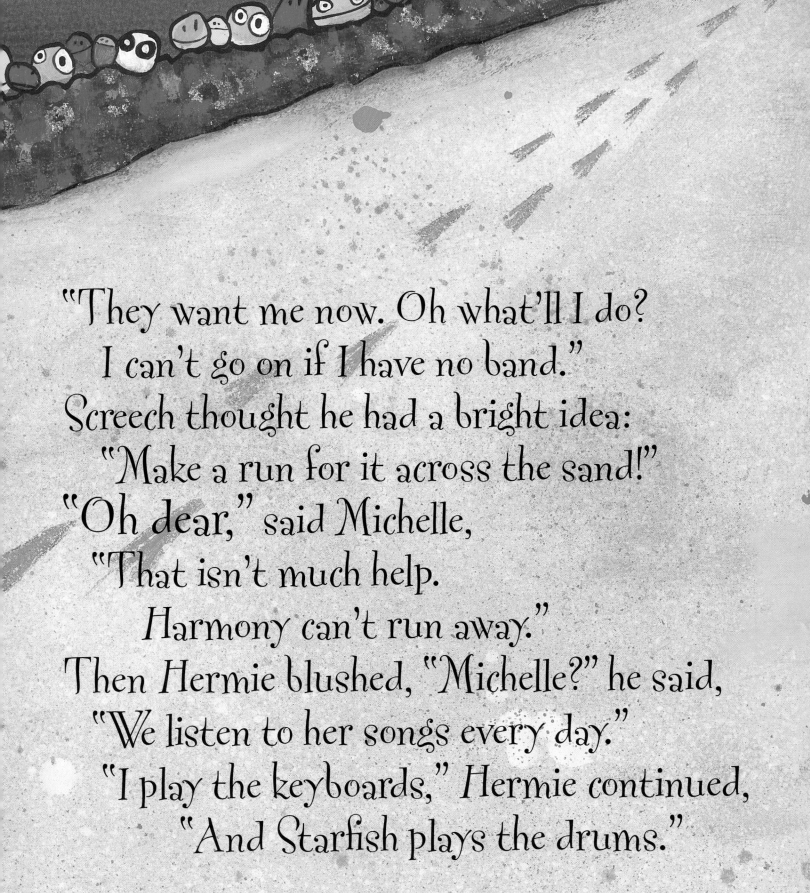

"They want me now. Oh what'll I do?
 I can't go on if I have no band."
Screech thought he had a bright idea:
 "Make a run for it across the sand!"
"Oh dear," said Michelle,
 "That isn't much help.
  Harmony can't run away."
Then Hermie blushed, "Michelle?" he said,
 "We listen to her songs every day."
 "I play the keyboards," Hermie continued,
  "And Starfish plays the drums."

"And I'm great on the air guitar.
I'm not all fingers and thumbs!"

Michelle thought for a bit then said to her friends,
"That's perfect but I'm afraid it won't do."
She turned to Harmony, "They can do it.
They're good. But are they good enough for you?"
Harmony's face dropped as Michelle went on,
"You see we have tried to help you all day.

But everything we've offered isn't quite right,
and you have told us to take it away."
Harmony knew what Michelle said was true.
She called, "Stop!"
before they could leave.

She really needed them to help her now, but
could she change and make them believe.
"I… I'm Sorry!" she spluttered surprising herself,
"I'm selfish and spoilt and rude.
I'm sorry I complained about the ledge and Screech,
the seaweed and the food.

I've been very silly and you've been so kind,
but please will you
lend me a hand?
You'd make this
day very special
   for me,
if you'd all be my
backing band."

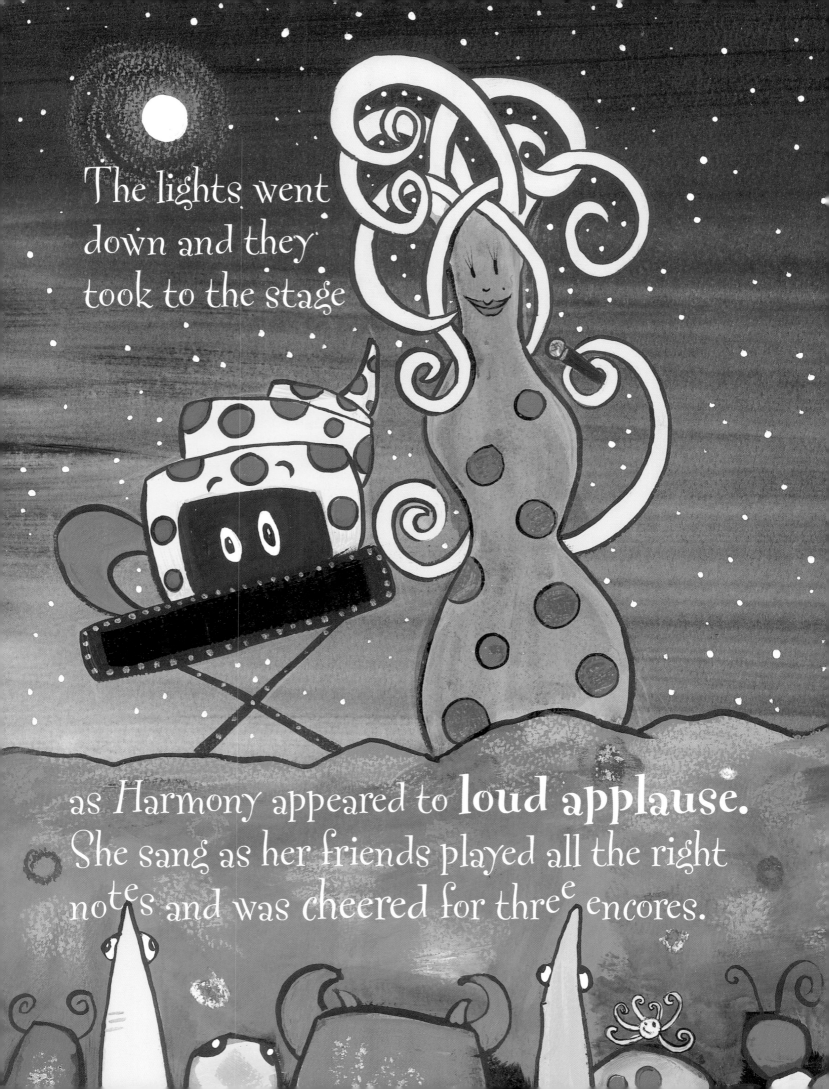

The lights went down and they took to the stage

as Harmony appeared to **loud applause.**
She sang as her friends played all the right notes and was cheered for three encores.

When they finished Harmony smiled
like she had never smiled before.
And for the first time in her life,
she knew what
friends were for.

Michelle The Rock Concert

would like you to know that full book size prints of the
pictures in this story-book are available online at

www.juliehegarty.com

Watch out for Julie's next book
in the Michelle series